Level 1

some initi   ld
very simp
repeated v

Special features:

Opening pages
introduce key
story words

clothes

woman

man

wife

boy

Emperor

Careful match between
story and pictures

The next day the man
came back.

"Do you like your
beautiful new clothes?"
he said. "Only clever
people can see them."

Large,
clear type

Educational Consultant: Geraldine Taylor
Book Banding Consultant: Kate Ruttle

A catalogue record for this book is available from the British Library

Published by Ladybird Books Ltd
80 Strand, London, WC2R 0RL
A Penguin Company

011
© LADYBIRD BOOKS LTD MMXI. This edition MMXIII
Ladybird, Read It Yourself and the Ladybird Logo are registered or
unregistered trademarks of Ladybird Books Limited.

ISBN: 978-0-72327-277-9

Printed in China

The Emperor's New Clothes

Illustrated by Marina Le Ray

woman

man

boy

6

wife

clothes

emperor

7

One day, a man came to see the emperor.

"I can make you some beautiful new clothes," said the man.

9

The next day, the man came back.

"Do you like your beautiful new clothes?" he said. "Only clever people can see them."

"Yes," said the emperor.

But he could not see any new clothes.

13

The emperor saw his wife.

"Do you like my beautiful new clothes?" said the emperor. "Only clever people can see them."

"Yes," said his wife.

But she could not see the emperor's new clothes.

The emperor saw a man.

"Do you like my beautiful new clothes?" said the emperor. "Only clever people can see them."

"Yes," said the man.

But he could not see the emperor's new clothes.

The emperor saw a woman.

"Do you like my beautiful new clothes?" said the emperor. "Only clever people can see them."

"Yes," said the woman.

But she could not see the emperor's new clothes.

The emperor saw a little boy.

"Do you like my beautiful new clothes?" said the emperor. "Only clever people can see them."

"No," said the little boy.
"You do not have any
clothes on."

"Oh no!" said the
emperor and he ran
all the way home.

29

How much do you remember about
the story of The Emperor's New Clothes?
Answer these questions and find out!

- Who comes to see
  the emperor?

- What is special about
  the emperor's
  new clothes?

- What does the
  little boy say to
  the emperor?